W9-BTQ-169

TWO NICE MICE

By Jennifer B. Gillis
Illustrated by Gary Krejca

BARRON'S

Table of Contents

© Copyright 2006 by Barron's Educational Series, Inc.

Illustrations on pages 21–23 created by Carol Stutz

All inquiries should be addressed to:
Barron's Educational Series, Inc.
250 Wireless Boulevard
Hauppauge, New York 11788
www.barronseduc.com

Library of Congress Catalog Card No.: 2005054857

ISBN-13: 978-0-7641-3295-7
ISBN-10: 0-7641-3295-4

Library of Congress Cataloging-in-Publication Data
Gillis, Jennifer Blizin, 1950–
    Two Nice Mice / Jennifer B. Gillis.
        p. cm. – (Reader's clubhouse)
    Summary: A group of bugs ride their bicycles to the new restaurant in town, "Two
Nice Mice," and try the special of the day. Includes simple facts about restaurants, a
recipe for Nice Mice treats, and word list.
        ISBN-13: 978-0-7641-3295-7
        ISBN-10: 0-7641-3295-4
        (1. Insects—Fiction. 2. Mice—Fiction. 3. Restaurants—Fiction.) I. Title.
II. Series.

PZ7.G4156Tw 2006
(E)—dc22

                                                                                    2005054857

Date of manufacture: 09/2009
Manufactured by: Kwong Fat Offset Printing Co., Ltd.
                        Dongguan City, China

PRINTED IN CHINA
9 8 7 6 5 4 3

Dear Parent and Educator,

Welcome to the Barron's Reader's Clubhouse, a series of books that provide a phonics approach to reading.

Phonics is the relationship between letters and sounds. It is a system that teaches children that letters have specific sounds. Level 1 books introduce the short-vowel sounds. Level 2 books progress to the long-vowel sounds. This progression matches how phonics is taught in many classrooms.

Two Nice Mice introduces the long "i" sound. Simple words with this long-vowel sound are called **decodable words.** The child knows how to sound out these words because he or she has learned the sound they include. This story also contains **high-frequency words.** These are common, everyday words that the child learns to read by sight. High-frequency words help ensure fluency and comprehension. **Challenging words** go a little beyond the reading level. The child will identify these words with help from the illustration on the page. All words are listed by their category on page 24.

Here are some coaching and prompting statements you can use to help a young reader read *Two Nice Mice:*

- **On page 4, "like" is a decodable word. Point to the word and say:**
  Read this word. How did you sound the word out? What sounds did it make?
  Note: There are many opportunities to repeat the above instruction throughout the book.

- **On page 6, "sign" is a challenging word. Point to the word and say:**
  Read this word. It rhymes with "line." How did you know the word? Did you look at the picture? How did it help?

You'll find more coaching ideas on the Reader's Clubhouse Web site: *www.barronsclubhouse.com.* Reader's Clubhouse is designed to teach and reinforce reading skills in a fun way. We hope you enjoy helping children discover their love of reading!

Sincerely,

Nancy Harris

Nancy Harris
Reading Consultant

Would you like a bite to eat?
I know a place you might like.

We can ride there on
our bikes.

See the sign?
It says, *Two Nice Mice.*
Come and Dine.

Tie your bike to this pipe.

We need a place for four.

Here is a place.
One of these nice mice will
wipe it for you.

Here is a menu.
Have you tried Ike's Surprise?

What do you think it is?

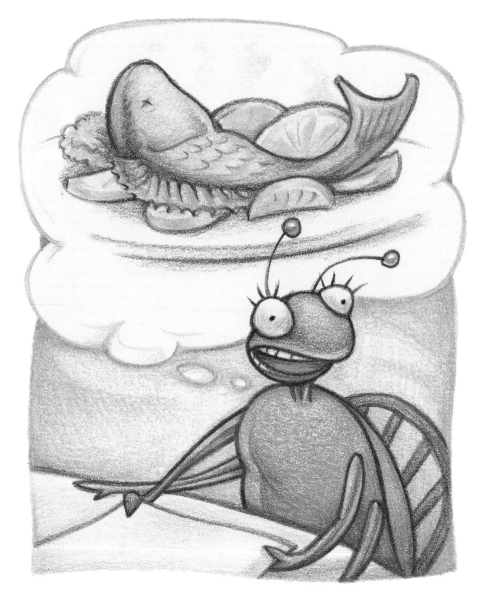

It might be cod with lime.

It could be fried rice.

We will have Ike's Surprise.

Look! The surprise is . . .
cheese!

How about a slice of pie?

No, thank you.
We are fine.

I am glad we have our bikes. We can take a nice long ride.

Two Nice Mice was quite a
fine place.

Fun Facts About
Restaurants

- The person who shows you to your table in a restaurant is called a *host* or *hostess.* In a very fancy restaurant, this person might be called a *captain.* Sometimes, the owner of the restaurant is the host or hostess.

- The people who take your order and bring your food are called *servers.*

- The person who cooks the food in a restaurant is called a *chef.* In big restaurants, a chef may have assistants. They are called *sous* (SOO) *chefs.*

- In some fancy restaurants, one chef makes all of the desserts. He or she is called a *pastry chef.*

- The person who cleans the tables after people have finished eating is called a *busperson.*

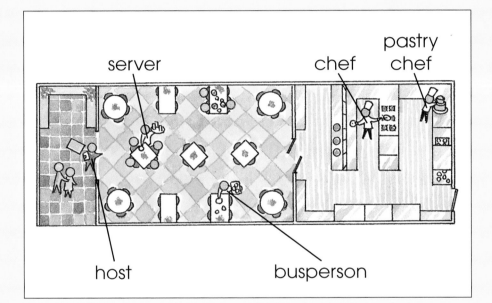

Nice Mice Treats

You can make nice mice treats for you and your friends. Ask an adult to help you.

You will need:

- 1/4 cup (59 ml) butter or margarine
- 6 cups (1.41 liters) crispy rice cereal
- 1/2 teaspoon vanilla
- small bag of miniature marshmallows
- chocolate chips or raisins for noses and eyes
- thin licorice strings for whiskers and tails
- wax paper

1. Measure 6 cups of cereal into a very large mixing bowl and set it aside.

2. With an adult's help, melt the butter or margarine in a pot over low heat. Stir in the marshmallows until melted. Take the pot off the heat and stir in the vanilla.

3. Pour the mixture over the cereal. Using a long-handled wooden spoon, stir until the ingredients are just combined. Cool to room temperature.

4. Make sure your hands are clean. Butter them to keep the mixture from sticking. Take about 1/2 cup of the cooled mixture in the palm of one hand. Form it into a mouse shape. Make several more mice and set them on wax paper.

5. Use raisins or chocolate chips for eyes and a nose. Ask an adult to cut up some of the licorice strings. Use pieces to make whiskers and a tail.

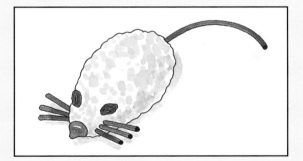

Word List

Challenging Words	menu	sign	
	might	surprise	

Long I Decodable Words	bike	like	quite
	bikes	lime	rice
	bite	mice	slice
	dine	nice	tie
	fine	pie	tried
	fried	pipe	wipe
	Ike's		

High-Frequency Words	a	how	the
	about	I	there
	am	is	these
	and	it	think
	are	know	this
	be	long	to
	can	no	two
	come	of	was
	could	on	what
	do	one	would
	eat	our	you
	for	says	your
	four	see	
	have	take	
	here	thank	